TROLL

A REAL KINGDOMS ADVENTURE

Also by Ross Kitchen

YA Publications

Allycyon, The Exiled Elf
Allycyon and the Wolves
Allycyon, The Raider due 2024
Allycyon and The Boar Hunt, due 2024
The Unlucky Adventurer (Maëlys, Book 1)
Maëlys and the Rogue Mage, due 2024
To Rescue a Princess, (Tatiana, Book 1)

Children's books

The Bored Princess

Copyright © 2023 Ross Kitchen

A catalogue record for this book is available from the British Library

ISBN 978 1 7384616 0 8

Printed in Great Britain by
Short Run Press Limited, Exeter, UK

The materials used to produce this book, have been sustainably sourced to
protect the future of our forests.

DEDICATION

To the School of the Sword, Swindon, for putting me in touch with Jon.

ACKNOWLEDGEMENTS

I would like to thank Jessica Wells for proof reading my manuscript. Thanks also go to Sharon from SRP, for the help she provided on how to correctly format a book.

6

TROLL QUEST

A REAL KINGDOMS ADVENTURE

Author

ROSS KITCHEN

REAL KINGDOMS CREATED BY

JON ABSON

CONTENTS

SCHOOL ON A MONDAY

School, according to some people, was the best time of your life. Though it also provided plenty of opportunities for it to be the worst as well.

As schools went, this one was an eclectic mix of styles and construction materials. The original block, which still fronted the main drive, was a Victorian, red brick, building. The lintels above the two main entrances still bore the deeply engraved signs for Girls and Boys, separate entrances for each, as required at the time. Two stories high, the block was now surrounded on three sides by later additions, designed by architects with a view to saving money, rather than providing a pleasing aesthetic.

Today, school started the same as it did every day for me, with Mum dropping me off at the gate. Blowing me a kiss, she yelled from the car. "Bye Jake. Be good and enjoy school."

She knew how much it embarrassed me in front of my friends, but much to my annoyance she still insisted on doing it every day. Waving bye, I rushed over to where my friends were pushing and shoving each other, a regular occurrence both in and out of school.

Ignoring the heckles about being a baby, or even a mother's boy, I just grinned back at them, joining in the pushing and shoving that just avoided going over into wrestling or fighting. No one wanted detention for having a dirty or torn uniform.

The weekend had been long and I was now glad to be back, kicking a ball around the playground with my friends.

Like most of my friends, I had a love, hate relationship with the school. I disliked having to go, but missed my friends when I didn't. School life was quite routine and boring, unlike that of my parents and grandparents, judging by the stories they told.

Here, there were no mass brawls with students from nearby schools; no noisy pupil strikes and no prefects chasing students through the corridors at lunchtime.

Bullying seemed to have not only been rampant in their time but openly carried out as well. In addition, it seemed to have been completely ignored by the teachers.

Sometimes though, I wondered if half the stories they told me were made up, as some of the stories seemed unbelievable.

Like the time the entire sixth form apparently decided to bunk off the same compulsory lesson.

Unsurprisingly this didn't go unnoticed and resulted in a dressing down in front of the whole school at assembly. No detentions though, which I thought was completely unbelievable.

I had been friends with everyone in our group since starting primary school, there were five of us in all, making a nice compact group. Vince was a short, blond haired boy, with blue eyes, who always brought a football along. It was Mo who was the real football expert, at least if you excluded Kate, but she is a girl and would rarely join in unless we really pestered her.

Mo was tall and lanky with black hair, brown eyes and fancied himself to be the next Peter Crouch. Kate couldn't be more different, short with light brown hair and blue eyes but she excelled at anything she put her mind to and was intensely competitive.

When you included the girls, our group came to a total of nine people. While I was the usual instigator for anything the boys were involved in, Kate was the leader of the girls.

When the weather allowed, we would all meet up in the local playing field after school. In general, that simply meant us boys kicking a ball around while the girls sat and chatted. Occasionally, Kate would run over and score a goal or prevent one depending on her mood or who had the ball.

I didn't think of myself as being anything special, being of average height, with brown hair and brown eyes. It was just that I had to be busy and active all the time, all of my friends said I had ADHD, but I just put it down to getting bored easily.

The rest of our group consisted of three girls and two boys. Jenny, who had brown hair and blue eyes, was the goth in our group, at least outside school.

Jenny's best friend was Sienna, a girl with black curly hair and brown eyes. She was funny and friendly but had a really combative nature if you did or said anything she considered wrong.

Rob was the biggest and loudest person in our group, blue eyed and sporting brown hair that was always expensively cut. She was also usually the instigator of any rough and tumble games we took part in.

Last but not least were the two twins, Brad and Theo, who both had brown eyes and black curly hair, although their hair cut was usually different.

Once in school, I headed for my first class. Our first lesson today was History and at the moment we were studying Saxons and Vikings, a subject which I enjoyed learning about.

"Saxons and Vikings are cool. They get to run around all day with swords and shields." I made my view known in class, which was noisy at first as we all settled down at our desks and opened the required text book 'Anglo-Saxon and Viking History'.

"Settle down!" Mr Harris had a commanding voice and we all stopped talking and faced forward.

"Now I have a surprise to announce before we get started on our course work. Friday afternoon, there will be an extended lesson which will take place in the IT suite. There, you will be playing a computer game, which is linked to the current theme of Vikings and Anglo-Saxons."

Smiling, he waited for a moment to allow the excited chatter to go on before again calling on us to settle down.

"Don't get too excited, it's a fairly simple game in which you play an early middle ages character. The game combines adventuring and town building in a vaguely, Anglo-Saxon/Viking setting. So expect your characters to be more rounded than in traditional computer game. All of you are expected to take part."

He glared round at all of us before carrying on. "The game also blends in well with our visit to a Saxon/Viking adventure site planned for the weekend. So I expect you all to be on your best behaviour between then and now as it would be a shame for anyone to lose out because they have a detention."

"History is actually one of the subjects I like, although some of the text books are boring. Learning about Vikings and Saxons and the battles they fought though, that is really interesting."

Then it was heads down as we all got stuck into our history lesson.

After History, there was little time to chat or play, except for lunch. The following days seemed to blur together as all of us counted down the hours until our game on Friday, and the trip on Saturday.

THE GAME

The IT Suite was a noisy place after lunch on Friday. Everyone was over excited, having been looking forward to this lesson all week. Today I was stuck sharing a desk with Kate, Mr Harris having moved everyone around. The game was going to be matched with a live experience at the weekend, where we would get the opportunity to dress as our characters and act out a Quest.

"Do you play many games?" I asked Kate, more out of boredom than in expectation of a full answer.

"A few, my dad let's me play on the PS. Minecraft obviously, but also FIFA PRO and some of his fantasy games, I usually play as an Elf Ranger." Kate's answer surprised me as she had never joined in any of our conversations about computer games before.

I didn't get to learn any more about the games she played, as Mr Harris walked in at that point and called for quiet. Since we were all interested in getting on with the game, no one played up today.

"The computers are all set up and the game is loaded and ready. A few things first. This is first and foremost a chance to look at early middle age environments. So while I hope you all enjoy this afternoon and the weekend, I will be asking questions next week. The questions will cover both the game and the weekend visit, so pay attention to what your character is, what you are doing and the environment you find yourself in." He paused for a moment looking around at us, something he did regularly, usually picking out the noisy ones.

"Accounts have already been created for you, so I am afraid you are stuck with your existing names." This resulted in a mix of groans and laughs, as well as some shouted comments.

"Yes, well, it seemed like the safest thing to do, given several well documented cases of silly names being chosen over social media." He stared at Brad while saying this, which wasn't surprising as he was the one who would usually call out silly comments first.

"So some rules for you to remember. Together with Miss Pearce, I will also be in the game to ensure you all behave reasonably well." There were good natured groans at this.

"The game consists of a mix of town building, crafting and fighting, essentially how life would have been over a thousand years or more ago. Fights of honour are allowed in the game, as at the time these took the place of courts for personal grievances."

Mr Harris looked around at us for a moment before continuing, though he still had our full attention. "Set piece battles are also likely, as this was a period in time when borders and kingdoms were being established. Just remember, this is supposed to be an educational exercise. If you try to turn your character into a murder hobo, I will switch off your PC."

After the giggling and whispering at that comment had died down, Miss Pearce read out some more rules while Mr Harris handed out sheets of paper that contained our login details.

There was a cheer as Mr Harris finally called out that we could log in to the game. Then it went quiet as we all concentrated on the screens in front of us.

Like all the others, I raced to log in, almost typing my name wrong in my hurry, I could hear faint groans around the room as others clearly ran into similar problems. Finally after logging in to the game, I was faced with a selection screen that looked like all those I had ever seen or read about.

In the centre there was a large image of a young man, dressed in loose trousers, tunic top and plain leather boots. He could pass muster as either a Viking or a Saxon, or pretty much any European from that age.

To the left of the screen there were options to pick a race, such as Elf or Dwarf.

To the right similar selections allowed me to choose, hair, skin and eye colour. The default was brown hair and blue eyes, so I changed the eye colour to brown to match mine.

"Now on to character creation, I am not really bothered too much, as long as it allows me to be a dual sword bearing, ninja."

The top left selection was Human and clicking on it didn't change anything about the central character other than make some words appear underneath. They weren't very exciting.

[Human, average height and build. No special affinities for weapons but can handle any weapon to expert level with sufficient training.]

Curious about the others, I clicked steadily through all of them, ignoring the hubbub around me as my friends all started to discuss which character they were going to choose and why.

[Elf, taller and slimmer than a Human. Athletic and dexterous. Lives in the forest. Affinity for plants and bows.]

[Dark Elf, taller and slimmer than a Human. Athletic and dexterous. Affinity for bows and poisons. Prefer to live underground and wear dark clothes to avoid the sun. Seen as cruel and Malevolent.]

[Dwarf, shorter and stockier than a Human. Strong but slower. Like mining, metalwork and jewels. Affinity for war-hammers and double headed axes.]

[Dakrak Dwarf, shorter and stockier than a Human. Strong but slower. Like mining, metalwork and jewels. Affinity for war-hammers and double headed axes. Dark Dwarves are only interested in wealth and are the only Race that Will ally with Orcs.]

[Orc, taller and stockier than a Human, strong and quick. Affinity for any chopping weapons, spears or spiked clubs. Prefer to live underground or in deep forest.]

I could hear some of the others discussing why there were fantasy creatures in a Viking, Anglo-Saxon setting. At the moment that didn't really bother me, as all I wanted to do was wield two swords like a ninja.

Sticking to that requirement though, really narrowed down my options so I chose Human. A tick box now appeared asking if I was sure, so I selected 'Yes' and the screen changed.

In the centre, the image of a young man was still there, but the options had changed. I now had another three choices.

[Imperial Saxon, average height and build. No special affinities for weapons but can handle any weapon to expert level with sufficient training. Automatically distrusts Norse.]

[Norse, average height and build. No special affinities for weapons but can handle any weapon to expert level with sufficient training. Automatically distrusts Imperial Saxons.]

[Outlander, average height and build. No special affinities for weapons but can handle any weapon to expert level with sufficient training. Automatically distrusted by Viking and Saxon]

"Why is setting up a character so difficult?" I muttered this to myself as I thought about the characteristics of each group and what I wanted for my character.

"Vikings and Saxons always fought in groups, all armed with the same weapons. Each would have a large round shield, coupled with a spear, sword or axe. If I want to have two swords, I will either need to be in charge so that I can do what I want or I will have to be an Outlander."

Further thoughts on my character's development were curtailed by a peremptory knock on the door followed by someone walking straight in. This not only stopped my progress, but everyone's as we all looked up to see who had entered the room.

HEADMASTER

Looking up to see who had interrupted our class, I was unsurprised to see the Headmaster, Mr Grumpton as he was the only one who never waited for an answer to his knock.

As he walked around the classroom, I had to hold back a smile as I thought of our nicknames for him. Generally, he was Mr Grumpy, as he was usually in a bad mood and it rhymed with his name. Other than that, he was nicknamed Batman, on account of the long black, teachers cloak he insisted on wearing as if this was still the eighteen hundreds.

Work stopped as he started talking to Mr Harris and we all listened in. "How come they all seem to be playing a game?"

"It is a game, but it is historically accurate and gives them a more realistic idea of life at the time."

Mr Grumpton seemed to scowl even harder at this. "I don't remember reading about elves and dwarves in my history lessons."

"The developers felt that giving it some fantasy elements would allow for a much broader uptake by students. It also leads into discussions about pre Christian religions and Norse sagas."

"I assume there are lesson elements involved beyond just playing the game?"

"Of course. It is all tied into the current subject matter, Saxons and Vikings. Further more, unlike most games, you are limited to human strengths and weapons and there are demerits for acting in an antisocial manner."

"I will be interested in seeing your report on this then." With that the Headmaster, who hadn't smiled once the whole time he was in the room, departed and we could all get back to playing our game.

The screen I was looking at, remained the same as before the interruption by the Headmaster. Making my choice, I quickly selected Outlander, as this option gave me the most versatility going forward.

Now I had to choose a class and once again there were multiple choices available to me, in total there were eight to choose from.

[Warrior. No special affinities for weapons but can handle any weapon to expert level with sufficient training. Wears the colours of selected Group.]

[Barbarian. Affinity for large weapons but can handle any weapon to expert level with sufficient training. Refuses armour.]

[Rogue. Likes to discover secrets, excels at moving stealthily. Affinity for scouting, ambushing and disabling traps. Uses, short sword, knives as well as magic]

[Bard. Support position. Magic, mayhem, and humour. Bards can entertain, heal and fight. Restricted to light armour, knives or short swords.]

[Ranger. Expert at hunting and tracking, use their skills to protect the borderlands. Can utilise most weapons and can also cast spells that harness nature.]

[Mage. Trained in magic, generally restricted to knives and staffs but can use any weapon in a push. Spells are kept in a personal spell-book. Warrior or healer, can be both but in that case spells and quantity will be weaker and lower than a specialist.]

[Cleric. Absolute commitment to deity of choice. Non-bladed weapons, such as Mace and Quarterstaff. Can use magic as a weapon or to heal.]

[Crafter. Adept at making anything. Can utilise most weapons and improvise loads more. Generally restricted to axes, knives and hammers.]

"Why isn't Ninja on the list?" I must have said this louder than I intended as Kate answered me with a laugh.

"Hundreds of years too early for Ninjas, Jake, and also the wrong continent."

Embarrassed at being caught out by Kate, I ignored her comment and carried on studying the choices available to me.

The only two that directly appealed to me and my desire to be ninja like were the Rogue and the Ranger.

Ninjas appeared to be a blend of the two. In the end, the ability of a ranger to wield two swords won out over sneaking around in dark clothes.

Sighing deeply, but pleased that I had finally finished the selection process, I selected Ranger and followed the prompts when asked to confirm.

Once again, the screen changed, this time dropping me outside of a village.

More than a dozen buildings could be seen through the open gates of a wooden palisade fence. All the buildings seemed to be similar, being constructed of wood, combined with wattle and daub, they were well spaced out and all featured thatched roofs.

Within moments, the entire class appeared around me, with Kate being closest. The first thing I noticed was that the characters of Mr Harris and Miss Pearce were much taller than any of us.

Kate, having just confided in me that she liked playing as an Elf in fantasy games, appeared unsurprisingly as an Elf, but she had also picked the Ranger class like me.

However, although she was dressed in the same manner as me, it was her hair and eyes that stood out, they were so different from real life.

She caught me staring and glared back at me. "What? There was nothing in the rules that said our character has to look like us. I have always wanted to have red hair and green eyes."

Looking away, I made a point of not staring at Sienna. Her character was also an Elf but a bard this time, with blond hair and blue eyes. Like Kate, she was scowling at everyone who was staring at her.

Mo also stood out, as his character was a solid looking Dwarf, Crafter. I couldn't resist asking why.

"I like building things," was his answer. This actually made sense as I had been to his house and it was full of models he had built.

"That was it, you just wanted to build things?" Rob asked.

"I wanted to fight as well, but at the same time, building things had to be in there. Blacksmith was the only craft option that let me handle anything larger than a knife."

Kate turned to me, smiling. "Why did you choose Outlander? I would have thought Warrior would have been closer to a Ninja."

"I did think about it but they all have shields and fight together. The main thing I wanted to do was wield two swords and be able to fight on my own, which left me choosing between Rogue and Ranger. Finally, I chose Ranger as I wanted to be able to use the longer swords."

Everyone laughed at my desire to be a ninja. There were lots of comments about turtle armour and eating pizzas. After that, we discussed everyone else's choice, although none provided the humour the reason for my choice did.

Looking around, I thought that the rest of our group made for a good team with a little of everything. Unsurprisingly, no one had chosen Orc, Cleric and Barbarian were also absent.

"Orcs are always seen as the baddies, so it isn't surprising that no one has chosen that option. The other two choices are just too specialised."

Vince was an Elf Warrior and matched Sienna with blonde hair and blue eyes. Jenny hadn't changed much, sticking with Human and brown hair paired with blue eyes, her character was a Mage Healer.

Rob, like Jenny had stuck to her real characteristics of brown hair and blue eyes, but was now a Saxon warrior. Brad and Theo had also stuck to their real characteristics of black curly hair and brown eyes. Brad was a Dwarf Warrior though while Theo had selected Human Mage.

If I concentrated on a person, details of their character sheet became visible, along with a notice saying that as I became stronger, I would see even more information.

Just as in the real adventure, which we were attending at the weekend, all of us had appeared just outside an early medieval village. We were stood on a path that led through open gates to the Chieftain's Longhouse. Our first action needed to be to enter the longhouse, talk to him and accept a quest.

THE VILLAGE

The village in front of us, consisted of a wooden palisade fence enclosing probably twenty to thirty acres. That might sound like a large area but you could walk around the outer wall in less than twenty minutes. Around two dozen buildings were scattered haphazardly, within the enclosed space.

From a set of double gates in the wall, a wide path led to the centre of the village, which happened to be the location of the largest building. This was the Longhouse of the local Jarl or Chieftain, a wooden dragon with open mouth, jutted out from just under the roof.

The remaining buildings all looked similar in design but differed in size and decorations. Some of the larger ones were protected by their own picket fence.

To one side of the village there was a small open air market which had a number of stalls, selling lots of items from fresh food to swords and shields.

The track led us up to the gates, where we passed two guards who simply nodded at us as we walked through, clearly used to seeing groups of adventurers enter the village. Mr Harris and Miss Pierce led us on through the village to the largest of the buildings, which had been built with its entrance facing the gates.

As we walked along, I could see chickens wandering around loose, while some of the fenced properties also had cows, pigs and sheep, judging by the sounds and smells.

"The smell reminds me of the dairy farm we visited, less overpowering, but more pervasive. How can people live like this? The animals are living in the houses with their owners."

That had been the biggest shock to me, in our current subject. At first, it had been amusing but the more I thought about it the worse the idea seemed.

Mr Harris and Miss Pearce knocked lightly on the Longhouse doors before leading us inside. It was dim and smokey, making me squint and cough at first, and several of my friends were doing the same.

As I became accustomed to the gloom, the features of the building started to stand out. It was smaller on the inside and a door in the back wall presumably led to other rooms.

Even with the window shutters held open, there wasn't much light, the shutters were small and high up, designed with preventing entry in mind rather than letting in air and light.

The windows themselves were simply holes in the walls, there was no glass and during the winter it no doubt became a very cold and drafty place.

Along both main walls, a row of three trestle tables provided seating for maybe sixty people. In the centre, a large hearth was the source of most of the smoke in the room. Lanterns and candles produced the rest while also providing additional lighting.

Now I noticed that there were three men at the back of the hall, one was seated, while two others were standing to the left and right of him.

The one in the middle was seated in a large chair that wasn't quite a throne but no doubt the carpenter had thrones in mind when he built it. With a sword, held across his lap and wearing trousers and tunic, his outfit was completed by a grey, wolf-skin cloak.

To his right, stood a tall, slim man, again dressed in light coloured trousers and tunic style top. On the left was another man and although he was dressed in the same fashion, of trousers and tunic top, his were all black, he also looked significantly older than the other two.

I almost jumped when the man on the not quite a throne spoke, as I was so lost in my imagination, fired up by what I was seeing.

"Hello fair travelers, welcome to my hearth and home. My name is Ragnar and I am the Jarl of this village and the surrounding area, and to my eyes you look like adventurers. If you are interested in a quest, I do have a new one available."

Mr Harris was still at the front and took over for us, matching the Jarl in using businesslike language. "We would be pleased to accept a quest from you. This will be their first adventure but I am sure they will all acquit themselves well."

"In that case, my Skald here has the details and can discuss them with you. In summary, a Troll is again raiding the area."

I was sure I heard a few words of complaint, although I couldn't pick out who said what. In turn, I may have said 'Rubbish' slightly louder than I intended, judging by the quick look Miss Pearce gave me.

"With all the options available, hunting for treasure, fighting Saxons, Vikings or bandits, we get landed with looking for trolls. I suppose it could be worse, we could be set to building walls or tending the fields."

Life could be so unfair, were my immediate thoughts and these were mirrored on the faces of all my friends as I looked around to see what everyone else thought of our choice.

Before we could complain, Ragnar, the Jarl or Chieftain, leaned forward and looked at all of us in turn. "A Quest is an important decision for heroes and comes with both responsibilities and the possibility of rewards."

That caught our attention, our scowls immediately replaced by smiles. Continuing on, the Chieftain now had a rapt audience. "The simplest rewards are Hero Points which unsurprisingly, you receive for acting like a hero. That means being gracious in defeat and victory, whilst also being a good sportsman. As an aspiring hero, you should also be thinking about how you can help and encourage your teammates, as a chain is only as strong as its weakest link."

He had been smiling while he spoke to us but now he had a much sterner look to him. "Don't forget though, Hero Points can be removed just as easily as they are given. If you are seen to ignore the rules or act in an un-hero like manner, you will be penalised."

Vince whispered to me. "What does penalised mean?"

I almost laughed at that, given his obsession with football, so quickly whispered back. "To be given a penalty."

He looked startled but didn't reply and once again I concentrated on the Chieftain.

"For a Quest well completed, I can be a very generous host, but I expect suitable evidence. My Skald here, Halvar will take your names and when you have finished he will record your story. Sometimes he will even accompany adventurers to record the story as it happens."

He paused then as a door to his left opened and closed noisily, allowing three people to enter.

The eldest was a blond girl, dressed in trousers and tunic, the hilts of two swords could be seen poking up over her shoulders, one on either side. She was chasing two young blonde boys.

A quick game of tag followed, much to our amusement, as she tried to grab both of the boys.

The two boys were avoiding her mostly by dodging under the tables. This was something the girl was unable to do easily or quickly, being taller and encumbered by the two swords sticking up over her shoulders.

However, she didn't seem to be disheartened by this, looking quite at home, whether vaulting over the tables or sprinting round them.

Now that I looked more closely, I was surprised to notice two hunting dogs lying down, one under each centre trestle table and therefore close to the fire and any cooking that may be going on. Both dogs were completely ignoring the two boys who occasionally climbed over them.

The game stopped when the girl finally managed to grab both, an event that brought a reaction from the Chieftain. "Inghram, Ingolf! That is enough, go back to your mother. I am in the middle of a business transaction here!"

There was some muttered agreements from both boys, before they left quietly, heads down and scuffing their feet. That meant they missed his smile.

"Brenna, as these are new adventurers can you please accompany them and help as much as you can."

The young girl had started to follow the two boys towards the door they had entered the Hall from, but at his call she turned around and walked over towards our group.

After that, the Chieftain turned his attention back on us. "Brenna is my niece and a proven shield maiden and will be invaluable to a new group like you. Torsten, my right hand man here, will help train and arm you. As that appears to be everything, let's see how well you do on this quest."

Mr Harris took that as the dismissal it was and bowed politely, indicating at the same time that we should do the same, so I bowed my head quickly and turned to follow the teachers out of the longhouse.

ARMOURY

Mr Harris and Miss Pearce called us all together and then led us to another wattle and daub building, following the lead of Torsten and Halvar.

There was no dragon protecting this building, instead it had Runes carved into the lintel above the door.

My imagination leapt to protective spells or curses but apparently they were obscenely normal and simply spelt out Armoury in Runic according to Halvar. Torsten opened the door into the armoury and then invited us all in, inside it was laid out much like a shop. A rack of weapons and shields faced us, together with chainmail hauberks, sheepskin jerkins and cloaks of various types.

More weapons were standing in oak barrels, placed strategically around the room.

Torsten started opening shutters to let in more light as we all started talking at once.

My eyes were immediately drawn to all of the swords. There were two types to choose from, short swords and what I considered to be normal swords, those with a long wide blade, that tapered steadily to a point and having a simple cross shaped hilt.

I picked up two of the longer swords and started to wave them around dramatically until yelled at by Mr Harris.

Calming down, I stood there quietly until Brenna came over, holding a belt and two scabbards, these clearly went around my waist unlike those she was wearing.

Laying both swords carefully on the ground, I took the belt and scabbards, fixing it around my waist and then looking it over to ensure the scabbards were evenly spaced on each hip.

Once the scabbards were fixed to Brenna's satisfaction, I carefully placed a sword in to each.

Of course, then I had to undo it, much to Brenna and Kate's amusement. Kate having finished her selection, had walked over and started talking to Brenna. The problem that had caused the humour? I had forgotten about the chainmail.

It didn't take long to fix the issue though and in moments I looked like everyone else, outfitted in chainmail and a sheepskin jerkin, my belt redone and both swords sheathed. My brown hair was kept short anyway and didn't need fixing in anyway.

The loops holding my scabbards to my belt were apparently called frogs and came in two sizes, the rear one being slightly longer so that the sword hung at an angle pointing down and backwards.

Standing in a line, so that Halvar could note down our choices, we must have looked an odd sight. Brenna and me with our dual swords. Kate as a tall slim Elf, with green eyes and long red hair, which was braided for the moment. Her weapons of choice were a bow and short sword, together with a dagger.

Mo, with short black hair and brown eyes was a Dwarf and had chosen a traditional war-hammer almost as big as him, together with a shield. How he expected to wield the war-hammer single handed, I didn't know.

Vince, like Kate was a tall, slim Elf, with blue eyes and blond hair. He was currently sporting a short pirate style ponytail. Together with a shield, he had selected a glaive, a type of spear which also had a long cutting edge like a sword.

Jenny, a human with brown eyes and brown hair kept in a short bob, was the shortest of our group and had chosen a bow and short sword.

Rob, was another Human, with blue eyes and short brown hair, she was wielding a sword and shield combination.

Sienna was another tall slim Elf with brown eyes. Her black curly hair was done up in dreadlocks and held back by a large hair band. She held a bow and short sword even though she was a mage. Brad, a Dwarf with curly black hair and brown eyes, had a shield and spear. Finally there was Theo, a Human who like Brad had Brown eyes and black curly hair, he had chosen a sword and shield combination.

TRAINING

Torsten took over once Halvar had left, he took us back outside, following a track that led around to the rear of the armoury. Here, a large, flat piece of land was laid out as a training ground. Straw filled dummies were held up by wooden posts at one end, while straw targets lined the the other.

"First things first, form a line with arms and weapons outstretched, make sure, you are not touching either neighbour."

With Kate and Brenna either side of me, there were large gaps between us, as I had drawn both of my swords, matching Brenna. Kate had followed along and drawn both her sword and dagger, leaving her bow strapped to her back.

Training was boring at first, a series of warm up exercises and stretches. Then I didn't have time to be bored as it became hard work.

Swords, while not particularly heavy, require a lot of stamina to wave them around for hours on end. We had to learn how to slice and stab with our weapons, as well as parry.

Shields on the other hand are really heavy, and holding one up for any length of time is exceptionally hard work. Torsten provided guidance on how to hold the shield and even use it as a weapon in close combat or melee.

After being instructed on how to handle our weapons, we were given the opportunity to try out our skills on a row of straw filled dummies. Attacking a straw filled dummy turned out to be great fun.

Torsten would call out instructions from the side which gave those of us waiting for our turn, a laugh. Mostly his instructions were to do with stance or how we held our weapon or shield.

Lots of Torsten's instructions actually made great sense but would require lots of practice to perfect.

"Remember the aim of the game is to strike your opponent while not letting them strike you in return. Rather than rush up to someone, pause outside of sword reach and then make short darting movements to strike out, making sure to get out of range before they can recover and strike back."

That sounded difficult and tiring, while his next helpful hint seemed to be no less tiring. "An alternative is to run or step around an opponent, striking out as you do. Keep to their shield side, making it difficult for them to strike back in return."

Everything we were being taught, seemed to revolve around a shield. When I next had the chance to talk to Torsten, I asked him about using two swords.

"Two swords can be quite the advantage once you get used to wielding them. Think of the sword in your off hand as a shield. It may be thin but it has a much longer reach than a normal shield, so you can keep your enemy further away. If you get really good, you can then start using either hand for offense." That was definitely what I wanted to hear.

It appeared that I was well on my way to becoming a ninja warrior, even if I was wearing Saxon/Viking armour and wielding European style swords.

Then curiosity once again got the better of me. The middle of the training ground was marked out into large squares with lines of cobblestones. "Torsten! What are the lines for?"

"Glad you asked. They are the next stage of your training. You will form pairs and spar with each while remaining inside a square. I will judge how well you are doing as well as giving advice where necessary. Just be aware that leaving the square once a fight has begun is an automatic failure." He seemed happy telling us this, before changing to a much sterner look and continuing on.

"They also serve a secondary purpose. Whenever a duel is called, this is where it takes place, in full view of the village."

His speech over, Torsten organised the initial pairings and then assigned each pair to a square.

Our bouts only lasted a couple of minutes but seemed much longer at the time.

In general, I performed better against those with swords and shields, being rather aggressive myself and able to get closer in. Those with spears or staffs, tended to be very defensive, using the greater length of their weapon to keep opponents away.

To say I was tired by the time the last bout ended would be to really underestimate how I felt. I was hot, bothered and dripping with sweat.

After our bouts of sparring against each other, and given time to eat, drink and recover, Torsten had us form up as a team.

This formation had shield holders to the front, with archers and mages to the rear. Then as training, we had to quickly get in to this formation at a shout from him, regardless of where we were and what training we were doing.

I could hear Mr Harris and Miss Pearce laughing the first few times, as we ran into each other and snagged our weapons on each other's clothing. It was great fun, although at the cost of again being very tiring.

Finally, Torsten declared that our training was over and bid us farewell as he headed off to the Chieftain's Longhouse.

OUT ON OUR QUEST

Having completed our training, Brenna took over and decided the first thing we should do was walk round the village. In the meantime, Mr Harris and Miss Pearce decided that they were going to stay in the village and await our return.

This really would be 'Our Adventure.'

The village wall was almost circular but followed the contours of the land, giving the wall a kind of wavy affect.

Led by Brenna, we completed a circuit of the the wall on the inside. The tracks were dry and in places had been upgraded with wooden boards. Mostly these were outside the buildings that had their own fences, so it was very easy to see who had the wealth in a village like this.

Everyone was friendly enough though, and waved or called out, as we passed by. It was strange though, seeing farm animals living in such close proximity to people, and the farmyard smell was everywhere.

Most men were wearing variations on trousers and tunic top and while linen and wool cloaks could be seen on the women, most men had wolf or sheepskin cloaks.

The children were dressed like the adults. Girls in long skirts or trousers and the boys in trousers or shorts. Several smaller children were running around naked.

Having finally reached the open gates, still guarded by two men in chainmail, we said goodbye and walked out into the countryside on our own.

The land around the village was cleared of trees for several hundred yards, where it then became open woodland. The trees were mostly deciduous: oak, elm, ash and birch predominating, meaning that the occasional different tree stood out handsomely.

Here and there a horse chestnut or tall conifer caught my attention. My eyes drawn to the differences. The air smelt of damp and rotting leaves, not unpleasant, unlike the farm smells of the village.

I was walking with Mo and Vince, all three of us were practicing with our weapons and probably not paying the surroundings the attention they readily deserved.

Kate was leading, alongside Brenna, when I heard her call my name. "Jake, stop messing around, we are supposed to be on patrol, looking out for danger."

I almost replied 'Why only pick on me?' but stopped myself in time, instead answering with a sullen "Yes, Miss" as if she was a teacher. Mo and Vince laughed and shoved me, but at least they stopped messing around and walked along, beside me, eyes scanning the undergrowth for anything interesting.

From time to time, Brenna would have us stop and then she would point out something she thought we would find interesting. Deer trails, badger sets, even mole hills were all pointed out and then described.

Having completed a circuit, Kate and Brenna struck out to the north-west, Brenna explaining how she knew the direction.

"The sun rises in the east, sets in the west and at noon it is due south. Remember to check your direction regularly, as it is very easy to get turned around in woodland."

Then she went on to explain why she was heading out this way. "Saxon lands are over to the South-East, Vikings to the north-east. They vie with one another and us for land and resources. To the the north and west, highland moors eventually give way to mountains. Dwarves, dark elves and orcs live there in a constant state of conflict over resources. They also have to compete with ogres and trolls."

"Do you ever meet any patrols or war-bands out this way?" Rob sounded nervous and was jerking her head around at every noise.

"Yes, all the time, that is why we all send out regular patrols, if we didn't then someone would simply take over and the border would move."

Now we were looping around steadily moving further from the village, while trying to cover as much ground from north to west.

CAMPING OUT

There were few villages out here but smoke could be seen rising from the occasional homestead.

"Who do the homesteads belong to?" What? I was curious about them.

"No one. A mix of Vikings, Saxons and others who prefer to be left alone, a harder life than in a village but they don't have to pay tax to anyone. The disadvantage is that there is no one to protect them should bandits or monsters come along." Now that had all of us perking up in interest.

"Have you seen any bandits or monsters?" Sienna beat us all to the important question.

"Yes, and Saxons and Vikings. Not here though, as I said, Viking and Saxon lands are to the other side of our Kingdom. These individuals sneak through our lands and set up as far from civilisation as they can get." Brenna didn't look too happy at the thought of these people slipping through their guards. Sealing a border though was a major undertaking.

"There is a Troll that comes around occasionally and has to be chased off, I assume this is the same one. I saw it the last time it tried to ransack our village." Now she paused for a moment lost in her memories of the event.

"As for bandits, they come through here regularly, especially at harvest time and towards the end of winter when everyone is short of food."

This was so cool and it took my mind off the long trek we were on.

Having reached about halfway to the moorlands, Brenna called a halt and had us make camp. Like everyone, I was glad to sit down and rest my feet.

Here the land was mostly free of trees and we were currently walking next to a large stream that had cut a ditch several yards across and a couple of feet deep. Reeds lined the edges and flashes of blue could be seen as Kingfishers flew by.

Rather than the expected ring of stones with a fire in the middle, Brenna had us build a fire-pit. This was a deep pit with a fire at the bottom, several channels supplied air, while the meat and any pots were supported at ground level. Three branches, still covered in leaves, met above the pit and broke up the smoke while also producing a pleasant aroma.

As we were building it, Brenna explained that there were several reasons for using a fire-pit rather than a standard camp fire.

With a fire-pit, the fire was below ground so it was difficult to see from a distance. Due to the chimney creating a strong draft, the fire burned hotter, and therefore produced less smoke. This helped reduce the visibility of the smoke column, something enhanced by the branches. All in all, a much more stealthy version of a standard camp fire.

We chatted about everything as we sat around the fire before Brenna called it a day. She was going to wake us up at dawn as we had a long day of hiking ahead of us.

Brenna proved true to her word and had us up to meet the sunrise.

This was a spectacle I had never really taken the time to look at before, even in the winter when I was usually up in time to view it. There was always something more to do than sit outside eating breakfast, watching the sun rise over the horizon. I had to admit it though, it was rather cool.

"Do you watch the sunrise every day." Kate directed this at Brenna but I was curious as well.

"No, too much work to do, mostly helping look after my cousins and then training with Torsten."

"You train every day with Torsten? That sounds like a lot of hard work to me." I liked waving my two swords around but spending hours a day practicing would make it feel more like work than play.

"Torsten says you can't train enough, and that two hours training a day is the minimum needed to excel in the use of any weapon." The determined look on her face immediately reminded me of Kate and it came as no surprise to me that they were getting on well.

"Torsten keeps pointing out to me that training with only one person is apparently limiting. Essentially I know how to fight Torsten, if someone comes along who fights differently, I will struggle at first until I work out his techniques. This is fine if we are practicing but would be a big disadvantage in an actual fight situation and therefore really dangerous."

"Can't you fight the others in the village." Kate made what seemed to me, to be a sensible suggestion.

"Yes, and I do. Unfortunately they were all trained by the same person who trained Torsten, so they all fight in the same manner."

"So to improve significantly you need to find a trainer who fights differently?"

"In a way, yes. Fighting is a whole mix of things, like technique, strength, speed and agility. How you mix and match those depends on your mentality and body, together with how your opponent fights. The more techniques or tricks you can learn, the better in general you will fare in a fight, whether that is simply sparring or a real life and death situation."

We talked some more before embarking on our patrol, which sounded so much easier and better than an all day hike.

The hike took us through rolling hills, from the heights we could see across the valleys.

Columns of smoke marking habitations, villages marked by a haze of smoke rather than noticeable columns. With Brenna's help, we tried to avoid any villages or individuals that were spotted. We were out here looking for a problem in the form of a troll after all. None of us wanted to get bogged down in village politics, which accounted for most honour fights.

Here, an honour fight took the place of courts and judges. While you could take your complaint to the Chieftain or even the King, most disputes were settled via fights. Both sides had to agree to the length of the fight, what weapons could be used and the outcome on winning, losing or even drawing. Most fights were only to first blood or a submission. Fights to the death were frowned upon, since that resulted in losing at least one fighter.

TROLL

By mid-afternoon, we finally found trouble. Kate, who was acting as our forward scout for the moment, was maybe a few hundred yards in front of us. At this point, she should have been much further ahead, looking for a good camp site. Instead she was waving at us frantically.

Seeing Kate waving wildly, had all of us racing forward to reach her as quickly as possible, then we all just stopped and stared at the sight in front of us. Four people were sat dejectedly in front of a still smoldering ruin that was once a home. The roof had collapsed at some point and now only ashes remained inside the blackened wall.

Around the house, planted vegetable gardens had been roughly dug through by someone who didn't care about gardens.

The troll immediately came to mind, I could easily see where he had pulled up swathes of plants.

While I was staring around at the devastated gardens, Brenna led Kate warily up to the small group of people still sitting there. The group consisted of two adults and two children and while Kate comforted the woman, Brenna started chatting to the man earnestly.

Quickly getting bored of just standing around, twirling my swords, while I was watching Kate and Brenna talk, I decided to take matters into my own hand.

Sheathing both swords but keeping a hand on each hilt, I moved away from the enclosure and started looking at the ground and surrounding plants. Moving in a circle around the enclosure, it wasn't long before the others joined me.

"What are you doing Jake?"

"Searching, obviously. The troll isn't here, so where did he go? He didn't go back the way we came or we would have seen him."

The evidence of his passing wasn't restricted to the ruined gardens. All of the family's animals had been slaughtered and in some cases ripped to pieces.

"Just how strong is this Troll? Neither Halvar or Brenna mentioned the Troll having knives or axes, which means he did all this using only his hands and teeth."

Now the others spread out, joining me in searching, as we slowly walked along in a widening spiral centred on the ruined house. It was Mo who finally found something interesting after several false alarms, all of which turned out to be deer tracks.

"Over here, this is the biggest footprint I have ever seen. It's huge." Mo looked really pleased with himself as we all crowded around him. He wasn't joking either, a huge footprint was visible in the soft ground. The bushes to either side also had evidence of damage where something large had pushed through without regard to either itself or them.

"Come on. He's gone this way!" Yelling to my friends, I set off in the direction the footprints led. The others followed me but voiced their doubts.

"Shouldn't we wait for Kate and Brenna to lead us?" Jenny was the most vocal of my friends in urging restraint.

"No, they are busy helping that family. It is up to us to track this monster. Mark our trail to make it easier for them to follow if you want to, but we are making quite the trail anyway."

Looking back, it was easy to see where we had been. None of us were trying to be stealthy at the moment.

Having found his trail, the troll was easy to follow, like us he was making no attempt to hide where he was going. The trail was easy to follow, consisting as it did of footprints, broken branches and smears of blood.

"Do you think the troll is injured?" Sienna asked a question that had also occurred to me.

"No, or at least I don't think so. There is not enough blood. It is more likely that he has taken some of the farm animals with him." I heard Vince say 'or parts.' but didn't get into that conversation, not wishing to upset or worry anyone.

Looking up though, it was easy to see what he was doing at the moment. He was simply following the valley and presumably looking for all the homesteads we had seen from the hilltop.

"This way! We need to catch up with him and then get around him so that we can drive him back this way, back to the mountains he came from." I wasn't quite running, but I was moving at a fast pace, the others following along behind.

For the next few hours, we hurried along the valley in pursuit of the troll. All the while, getting steadily closer, judging by the fact we could soon hear him crashing through the woods in front of us. During our chase, we had passed two more destroyed homesteads, stopping briefly to check that each family was okay before racing on.

"If we catch up with this Troll, what are we going to do? My legs ache and I am out of breath." Rob did have a point.

I was struggling as well but having started, I didn't want to admit defeat and give up. Besides from what I could remember of the smoke we had seen, there was a village coming up.

"There should be a village up ahead." I yelled as I ran on ahead, immediately forgetting all the training we had gone through.

Coming out of the woodland we were traveling through, brought us to a large piece of relatively flat ground with a wide stream running across it.

The village was a few hundred yards away behind some planted fields and on the same side of the stream as us. The other side of the stream contained more planted fields and a few animal enclosures.

In front of us was the reason for our Quest and the cause of all the anguish we had seen on the way here, a very large troll.

Currently the troll was sat down and helping itself to food from the plots laid out in front of the village wall.

Alongside a large wooden club which could be seen laid on the ground next to him, the troll also had a large sack into which he occasionally threw something.

He looked immensely happy with himself as he chewed on what looked like the haunch of a sheep or goat.

The Troll was quite a sight. With his disfigured face, tombstone teeth and over long arms he looked less human than even a green skinned orc.

To make things worse, his chin was stained red with blood, as were his clothes and hands. All in all, the troll made quite the grizzly sight.

I could see people looking over the wall at us, some were waving, others just looking on stoically.

Presumably they were wondering whether we were here to help or were just another problem that they would have to face.

BATTLE

"Brad, Vince! You two run up and stab the troll to get its attention. The rest of us will circle round so that we are between it and the village."

"Who put you in charge? More importantly, why should we go and grab its attention? Shouldn't we just wait for Brenna, after all, she is the expert." Brad was always the most argumentative person in our group, always finding fault, regardless of what it was or who had put it forward.

"Just trying to make the most of things Brad, while Brenna and Kate are dealing with the casualties. Neither will be happy if they reach here and find us just sat around twiddling our thumbs and we won't gain any hero points. As to why you two, that is easy, you both have spears, while the rest of us have swords and knives."

Splitting into three groups, we put my plan into action. Brad and Vince, forming a group on their own, started to move in on the Troll.

The rest of us split into two groups and moved around the monster, forming a rough C shape with our backs to the village wall. We left a long gap between our two groups, Brad and Vince would each run to the outside end of an arm of the C having first caught the attention of the troll.

"Hopefully the troll is intelligent enough to see the issue with the gap between our two groups. If he attacks one group, the other will attack him from behind. If he gets stuck in the gap, then he will be completely surrounded and those on the wall can attack him from above. With a bit of luck, he will simply turn around and run, especially as I really don't want to get hurt fighting him."

I fervently wished that my thoughts on the troll would come true. Visions of the animals he had slaughtered were still vivid in my memory.

There was a loud roar as the troll was injured by the two spear wielders, the cuts were nothing more than scratches but still, they had to sting. Looking over to check on his reaction, I could see that he had stood up and was now waving his wooden staff around in an angry manner, yelling all the time.

To my surprise, he didn't just rush at us. Instead he took a couple of steps forward, stopped and screamed at us, while waving his arms. He then repeated this process, getting ever closer but staying between both our groups.

"It looks like he is trying to scare us, make us run without actually getting in to a fight. Didn't I read somewhere that lots of animals do that, to reduce the risk of getting life threatening injuries?"

Standing fully upright, the troll was an awe inspiring sight. Approaching eight feet in height, he carried an even taller staff, which looked more like a tree trunk than anything else. Regardless of its origin, it had to be close to twelve feet long.

Making him look even more fierce, if that was possible, there was blood smeared across his face and down his rough and worn clothes.

Looking at him, I could feel my heart rate increase at his approach, sweat was now dripping down my face and my hands were wet, so every now and then I was forced to sheath a sword to wipe my hands on my trousers.

It was Brad who acted first though. With a loud yell, he ran at the Troll, ignoring the plan entirely. His first stab got in under the wild swing of the Troll's club.

However, he wasn't quick enough with his second attempt and the back swing caught the side of his head as he ducked wildly out of the way.

Seeing Brad falling down, we had little choice but to go on the attack. Yelling loudly, we rushed to where Brad lay on the ground, unmoving.

Getting there, we had feared the worst and although there was blood in his hair, he was now groaning and trying to sit up groggily. As two of our group grabbed him under the arms and dragged him away, the rest of us tried to fend off the troll the best we could.

The troll slowly stepped forward, swinging his club in front of himself as he tried to clear us away.

We fell back steadily, keeping the wall on our left, hoping to surround him or force him to run.

Much to my delight, I managed to cut him twice. Dodging to his side, I slashed out with my right arm and then followed through with a back slash from my left arm. Both attacks connected and drew blood.

"That was so cool, dual wielding is the best. Admittedly, I didn't do much more than scratch him but apart from Brad, he hasn't hit any of us either."

Having found my group too difficult to fight, he spun around and attacked our second group just as they were creeping up on him from behind.

Now it was Vince's turn to lead the attack, sticking to the plan and making short runs, trying to stab the monster as the rest of his group formed a line behind him.

Like us, the troll was clearly worried about getting trapped, and now he was visibly worried, he kept swinging his head from side to side, looking at each group in turn and also occasionally glancing up at the wall.

The village defenders though, had contributed nothing to the fight so far. Whether that was from indifference to our plight or a desire not to rile the Troll in case he won, I couldn't tell.

With one final roar, spinning round completely with his club extended as far as possible, he cleared a wide area around himself.

This was the perfect opening for our mages and archers, who let loose with a hail of arrows and fireballs. This time, much to our relief, there was also action from the village. Archers and mages on the wall joined in, sending a third volley of arrows and fireballs towards the troll.

Crouched down to avoid the storm of arrows and fireballs being sent his way, the troll let out one last scream, turned and took off at a run towards the north-west.

A big smile broke out on my face. "We did it! We forced him to run away. Come on, we have to follow him, to force him back up into the mountains. If he finds somewhere to hide, we will have to go through all this again tomorrow."

To cheering and clapping from those on the village wall, we all took off at a sprint after the troll.

We slowed down almost immediately, quickly realising that we were tired out from our previous hike and race. We were also worried that if we became strung out, the troll could easily double back and pick us off one by one.

Brad was also struggling to keep up, even though he no longer seemed groggy and the bleeding had stopped. All things considered, there was no reason for us to continue on as a full group.

The troll could be seen and heard in front of us, still heading roughly north-west, terrain permitting and keeping up a blistering pace.

"Jenny, Sienna, Theo. Can you follow him, and let loose occasionally, keep him worried and running? Don't get separated from each other though, we don't want him catching any of us on our own."

The occasional arrow or fireball from our group, did indeed keep him honest and heading steadily north-west.

After another hour, I called a halt to our chase. It was early evening and we were all clearly exhausted.

"That's enough, I think. Everyone's tired and we also want Brenna and Kate to be able to catch up to us before it gets too dark." I was still elated with the success of our action against the troll and even Brad's action couldn't dampen my spirits as we stopped.

"That was amazing, and I liked being in charge and giving orders. More importantly, I got to fight like a Ninja, with two swords."

OVERNIGHT

We didn't stop, immediately. Scouting around first, for a decent camping spot. Having found one, we then made haste to prepare it, as no one likes putting up tents in the dark.

Kate had organised a roster for camp duties and I saw no reason to ditch it, simply because she was not here to enforce it.

"Brad, Theo. Your turn to collect firewood. Jenny, you are with me for the first nightwatch."

With a small group like ours, having one person on guard would usually be enough, but with the troll around, we all thought it would be safer with two.

Once our camp had been set up completely, Sienna and Jenny both stood up and started to head out to the woods we could see over to our left.

"Where are you two going?" There was safety in letting the group know where you were going when out in the wilds, I wasn't simply being nosy.

"Target practice with our bows, if we are lucky we might even bag a rabbit or two." Jenny seemed a little bit squeamish at that comment but Sienna had a broad grin on her face.

"Good luck then. Just don't get complacent, there are other problems out there besides our troll." Then I started to list them one by one, taking a perverse pleasure in seeing their faces blanch.

"We have still got wolves, bandits, vikings and saxons to worry about. Not to mention other monsters."

"Okay, we get the point, we will be careful." Sienna's cheerful demeanour had started to return as she punched me on the shoulder as a method of saying goodbye.

It was over an hour later before they returned, Sienna carrying a brace of rabbits in her right hand. Then came the hard part, preparing a rabbit. None of us knew what to do exactly, and Brenna had not yet arrived, so we couldn't simply hand them over to her to deal with.

For some inexplicable reason, I found myself shoved to the front with Sienna, the rest staring gloomily at the two dead animals.

It was a difficult, messy job but in the end we had our two animals roasting over the pit-fire that had been set up. The smell of roast meat quelling any queasiness about the source, as hunger took over our senses.

Brenna and Kate arrived as we were finishing off our meal. Being good friends, we had preserved some, wrapped in leaves ready for when they arrived.

We all stood up as they entered the camp and somehow, I again found myself being pushed forward. Glancing back at my now smirking friends, I started to explain what we had been doing.

"Hi, we followed the troll all the way to a village then chased him away to here. What happened to you two? We thought you would have been here ages ago."

Brenna didn't answer my question, instead she sniffed the air happily. "Roast rabbit, nice. Did you leave any for the two of us?" Thrown by the direction of the question, I turned a puzzled look towards Kate.

"As condensed versions go, Jake, that one takes some beating. Both of us are hungry though, so rabbit, wherever you got it from, sounds amazing."

Now I was confused by Kate's comment, as I had provided a clear statement of our actions to the pair of them. It reminded me of school where teachers were always asking me to expand on my answer, even though it was clear that I had understood the question and had answered it correctly.

While Brenna and Kate sat down and enjoyed their meal. I explained in more detail what had happened since we parted. Sienna and Jenny had also joined us and added their own flavour to the story.

Once the two of them seemed happy with my tale, I quizzed them on their actions, at which point Brenna deferred to Kate, saying it was our adventure and that she was just helping out.

Kate's voice was quiet at first, which was unusual for her. She picked up quickly as her confidence returned though. "We saw all of you wander off but felt we couldn't just up and leave that poor family. Once the initial shock had worn off, they were angry at the troll but thankful we had turned up to help, even if we were too late to save their house."

"They weren't angry with us for being late?" That seemed like a reasonable question and also a fairly normal reaction for someone in their position.

"No, maybe they were still in shock to some extent. Either way, they accepted our offer of escorting them to the village. It seems they didn't know about trolls, monsters and bandits plaguing this area." Kate joined Brenna in shaking her head at the stupidity of some people in not bothering to ask the local villagers about the area.

"Thank you for the trail markings by the way. It made our job of following you that much easier. The owners of the other homesteads all chose to follow us to the village. They were more fatalistic about their loss, and were clearly aware of the risks they took in living outside the village."

"What will happen to them now? Will they simply move into the village where it is safer?" I grew impatient with Kate's slow story telling.

She frowned at me for the interruption "No, they are all staying as guests of the village Chieftain. Starting tomorrow, the villagers will help all three families rebuild their homes. They were a friendly bunch and were really thankful for the help you provided in chasing off the troll."

Once again, I found myself smiling at the outcome of the quest. I had certainly enjoyed myself.

SOLUTIONS

Morning dawned cloudy and grey but thankfully, the promised rain never arrived.

We started off early, heading north-west as before. The troll was only veering from the direction when obstacles blocked his way. By mid-morning we had travelled far enough to realise he wasn't turning round and wouldn't be back any time soon. He was still heading roughly north-west towards the mountains and was not making any attempt to hide his trail.

At that point all of us were glad to be able to settle down for a well earned rest. Sitting down, eating trail rations, we fully relaxed for the first time since accepting the quest.

The thought of running into a large group of trolls, orcs or dwarves, if we headed even closer to the mountains was another key reason for giving up on the chase.

Now we were sat around discussing our options. The majority wanted to head straight for the village but Kate, Brenna and myself wanted to scout around here for a bit.

"You never know, we might discover some abandoned treasure." The thought of treasure swayed the others in my favour.

Our camp was by a small river that meandered through the wide valley we had been crossing. Willows and other trees lined the banks, reducing visibility noticeably.

It was was Rob who turned the conversation towards future plans. "How come no one lives here?"

"Too far from the main centres. Even patrols rarely come out this way. Trappers and traders swing through now and then but there are no major settlements out this far." Brenna answered easily.

"You could set up some way stations here, create vegetable gardens, that would help the trappers and traders and they needn't be permanently manned."

Like me , Jenny was staring around at the unused land all around us.

"That's not a bad idea, it would help prevent trolls and bandits heading deeper into your territory." Kate was clearly examining the idea in more detail than the rest of us but then again she was always top in tests.

"Actually you could go one better than that. Build a dyke along the hills behind us. That would keep out most of the monsters and bandits." Mo was clearly enlivened by his idea to build something big and was now stood up, staring at the low hills behind us.

"Aren't dykes used to keep back water?"

"Yes, but I was thinking more along the lines of Offa's Dyke. It consists of an earthen rampart, with a ditch in front of it, and runs for over eighty miles. If you build even a small one, by adding a palisade fence to the top, then anyone trying to scale it, is looking at an eighteen foot wall from the bottom of the ditch." Mo sounded breathless with excitement by the end of his description.

"Mo's Dyke! Sounds really impressive." I wasn't sure if Sienna was being sarcastic or not but the comment didn't seem to bother Mo.

For me it was easy to imagine such a wall on the hills behind us and I was impressed by the scale and Mo's determination to build things.

"I will certainly pass on all these ideas to my uncle, they sound different and better than anything put forward so far." Brenna sounded excited by all the ideas and like the rest of us was now staring intently at the low hills that Mo had pointed out.

REWARDS

Having made the decision to stop following the troll and failing to find anything even remotely resembling treasure, Brenna eventually had us turn around and head in a more or less direct line back towards her village.

I was tired out, the excitement of the chase having evaporated now the quest was over. Like most of the others, I was just trudging along now, relishing the relief I knew a sit down would bring.

Camping out overnight again, seemed to refresh me though, and I was full of bounce after getting dressed in the morning, which pleased some but annoyed others. Keen to be going on, I chivvied the others to hurry up.

Brenna had given Kate and me some extensive directions during breakfast due to the fact that we were both Rangers.

Having given us our instructions, she had then sent us on ahead of the main group as a pair of scouts. I thought that this was really cool, although Kate quickly tired at my attempts to move stealthily which admittedly did slow us down at first.

Scouting out in front of our main group, we were looking for any trouble that could engulf the team and also marking the easiest route.

After a while, I grew bored and started counting animals and trees, keeping up a running commentary with Kate. This then quickly evolved into a fun competition between the pair of us.

Finally we came in sight of the village wall and sat down to wait for the others to arrive.

Our competition had to be declared a draw at the end, which annoyed and pleased both of us in equal measure.

The reason for this was simple, we both had highs in some categories and lows in others. Despite quite a bit of discussion, neither of us could come up with an easy and fair weighting system, which would allow us to come to an agreeable total.

Once the rest of the team had finally caught up, we formed up in a half way decent column and marched towards the open gate and its two guards.

As it was late evening, there were very few villagers around to see us march up to the Chieftain's Longhouse. Brenna knocked peremptorily before opening the door and walking in. Looking warily at each other but having little choice in the matter, we followed Brenna in.

Mr Harris and Miss Pearce were sat together at one table eating a meal with another woman and the two blond boys we had seen before.

Ragnar was sat at the table opposite them, together with Torsten and Halvar. With them were several warriors, while more warriors were scattered in small groups across the remaining tables.

Seeing us enter, Ragnar stood up and called out to everyone, "I see our adventurers have returned. Come and sit here, there is plenty of room."

He waved at the men sitting with him and all but Torsten and Halvar got up and moved to another table.

I found myself sitting next to Ragnar, simply because no one else wanted to.

Kate was sat next to me while Brenna was sat next to Halvar and was already deep in conversation with him, Halvar scribbling down notes on pieces of parchment.

"So, how did your first quest go? Did you enjoy it?" Since I was sat next to him, Ragnar directed his questions at me.

"It went really well and I had a great time, I really enjoyed it." I heard Kate groan beside me, so turned to look at her, as did Ragnar.

"You really suck at answering questions, Jake. Ragnar, he means it was an honour being able to take part in one of your quests. The training we received, and the aid from Brenna allowed us to complete it successfully and in a much shorter timescale than expected. We had a fantastic time here and look forward to visiting again."

Ragnar laughed as I covered my eyes and groaned in turn.

"How am I supposed to come up with flowery language like that? It's hard enough, coming up with the answers I do."

"You are like Brenna, intelligent and independent. Don't ever let anyone tell you there is something wrong with that." Now it was Kate's turn to suffer, as I saw her blush at the praise from Ragnar.

Ragnar then turned to face all of us. "Together with Brenna, Torsten and Halvar, I will discuss the progress you have made on this quest. This will allow you to eat your evening meal in peace. Afterwards, I will talk through any rewards with you."

All three then left the room, closely followed by Brenna.

Turning to Kate, I asked the question I thought all of us would like the answer to. "What do you think Kate? Did we do enough to earn hero points or even treasure?"

"We completed the quest, that has to count for the most. Above that, we helped the distraught homesteaders and you took charge when you didn't have to. Actually, why did you do that?"

"To be honest, I was getting bored, and I also wasn't looking forward to being yelled at by you and Brenna, when you eventually turned up and found us all sat around like idiots." Kate laughed at that, but was prevented from replying by the arrival of our evening meal.

Several servants carried over plates of food for all of us, from the central fireplace and the room quieted down as we concentrated on filling our stomachs.

The food was a simple stew, served in a bowl and accompanied by fresh baked bread.

Ragnar returned just as we were finishing up. The bread dipped in gravy was delicious and now I was so full, I couldn't eat another thing.

Ragnar remained standing in front of his throne like chair, as Halvar and Torsten stood to either side of him, as they had when we first arrived. Brenna came and retook her seat with us.

"Having talked to my advisers and Brenna, I don't think I will waste any more time as no doubt you are all anxious to hear my decisions regarding your performance." He looked at all of us in turn with a stern expression on his face, which was quickly replaced by a smile.

"You all did very well. The troll has been sent packing and you helped the homesteaders move to the village, somewhere safe to stay while their homes are rebuilt." He paused for a moment, which allowed Halvar to pass him a small leather pouch.

"I guess you are all wondering, what kind of reward I will hand out for the completion of this quest. These are bracelets that show you have completed a quest to my satisfaction." Ragnar handed out a number of bracelets to Halvar and Torsten.

"There are four types of bracelet, leather, bronze, silver and gold. Which one you receive, depends on how well you completed the quest and how many hero points you amass." Like my friends, I was struggling to contain my excitement as Ragnar paused.

Brad was the first one called up by Halvar, who clearly had a list he was reading from. Walking up to the three men, Ragnar held his hand out for Brad to shake.

"In all you achieved three hero points, it would have been more but you lost some due to acting selfishly. Treat this as just a minor setback and determine to come back and do better next time." He then directed him to Torsten, who handed him a bracelet before shaking his hand as well.

Brad didn't look very happy, and I couldn't blame him, no one likes being singled out for punishment, especially in front of friends. On the other hand, we were warned in advance about losing hero points, which was one of the reasons I didn't want to sit around and wait for Brenna and Kate to arrive and tell us what to do.

Halvar then called out for Vince, before steadily working his way through our group. Most received five hero points. Mo was the first to receive more.

"Due to your idea of building a fortified wall along our border, I have given you six hero points. As the construction of such a wall is a huge undertaking, and would involve numerous villages and Chieftains, I will be taking your idea up with the King. If he approves the idea, you will receive more points."

Jenny and Sienna also received six for going hunting without being asked.

Without exception, they all received a plain leather bracelet with runes stamped deeply into the material.

"Only Kate and me left now. I hope we both did well."

Halvar called both of us up at the same time, something that struck me as odd.

"Since you two seemed to do more than absolutely necessary, I have decided that bronze bracelets are a suitable reward." Both of us mumbled 'Thank you' as we received our gift, a bronze bracelet, once again engraved with runes. It was also clearly more expensive than the leather bracelets everyone else had received.

"As you both did more than required, I have also decided to recognise this by awarding you both eight hero points each."

Ragnar had carried on talking but I missed most of it lost in my thoughts, catching up as he wished us well. "You are a good group of adventures, keep together and return again for another quest. You are free to leave whenever you want."

FALLOUT

Walking out of the longhouse, Torsten led us over towards the Armoury. On the way, Brad gave Theo a harder than usual push, almost causing him to fall over. Even I could see that Brad was in a bad mood, something I could partially sympathise with.

Since the brothers occasionally got far rougher with each other than anyone else, I left them to it, aware the teachers would step in if things looked like getting out of hand.

Except events spiralled far quicker than that. From shoving and shouting Brad suddenly called out "I challenge you to an honour duel!"

Torsten stopped immediately and turned to face Brad and Theo. "There are strict rules about honour duels. Having challenged someone to a duel, you must specify the reason and the penalty for losing, either by default or through combat. The challenged party gets to set the terms for his victory, which should match that of the accused in terms of value. Both sides must agree on weapons, they have to be the same and shouldn't give one party an undue advantage."

Both Brad and Theo looked confused now which almost had me laughing. It was clear that Brad hadn't thought this through but then he never did.

Brad finally looked up at Theo. "The reason is, not supporting your flesh and blood. The penalty for losing is having to do what I say on the next adventure."

"Do you accept these conditions Theo?" Like the rest of us, Theo could clearly see that we might be here for hours as the pair of them went back and forth trying to reach an agreement. So instead of arguing, he simply nodded his head to denote his acceptance.

"What are your terms for winning?" Theo looked surprised, as if he had forgotten that part of Torsten's description of the rules, mentioned only moments ago.

"The reverse then, Brad must follow my orders during our next adventure. As to weapons, I choose swords as we chose spear and quarterstaff, these will disadvantage us both equally."

Brad stared at his brother for a moment and then nodded his head. Torsten led us around to the rear of the armoury again and over to one of the marked out squares we had used for sparring.

"As I mentioned before, these squares are also used for honour fights. The rules are simple. You have to remain in the square until a result is declared. No one else is allowed in the square after the start. No one is allowed to provide help or advice at any point during the duel. Finally, the fight ends at first blood, calling out 'I surrender' or being forced out of the square. In the event of a tie, the challenge is declared null and void and can't be repeated within a year."

"Brad would simply come up with a new complaint." I whispered to Kate, which had both of us struggling not to laugh.

Torsten came up to me. "Can I borrow both of your swords, please?"

Unsheathing them one at a time, I hand them to Torsten, only to see him hand one to Brad and the other to Theo. He then repeated the process with shields.

When he was happy that both of them were outfitted correctly and equally, Torsten stepped out of the square.

"You are free to start whenever. Remember, this is only to first blood, a submission or removal from the square."

I was impressed at how slowly Brad started out. He was usually the first to jump into any rough and tumble play we came up with. Not surprisingly he suffered from repeated injuries because of this.

Both were circling slowly around each other, making quick feints and trying to force the other into a mistake.

It was clear that they were also worried about stepping out of the square, as both kept taking wary glances behind.

Brad finally decided to go all out and made a concerted effort to slash Theo.

Theo retreated steadily, keeping to moving in a circle as he tried to defend against the continued strikes from Brad, using both his shield and sword as he desperately tried to stay in the fight.

"Brad's blown it." I whispered to Kate, who was stood next to me.

"What do you mean?" While not taking her eyes of the fight between our two friends, Kate replied to my comment with a question.

"He always does this, goes mental for a moment and then collapses in a heap. Theo only has to last a little while longer."

True to my comment, Brad suddenly came to a shuddering stop, bent over and taking deep breaths as he tried to prevent a full collapse.

After a moment's indecision, Theo carefully approached Brad, obviously suspecting a trap. With no change in Brad, Theo carefully scratched Brad's neck with the tip of his sword, something that didn't even elicit a response.

Torsten walked over and checked Brad carefully, before smiling. "Theo, the Gods favour you today, so I confirm you have won this honour fight, and Brad will have to follow your orders during the next adventure you both take part in."

Still smiling, Torsten took the sword and shield from Brad, who still seemed to be in a daze. Kate and Sienna rushed over, followed at a slower pace by the rest of us.

"Is Brad okay?" Sienna sounded really concerned.

"Yes, he is just exhausted. Over exerted himself, the bane of all Berserkers. He will be fine after resting and having something to eat and drink."

Leading us back to the front of the armoury, Torsten opened the door and then stood back as we entered.

Taking off our cloaks and armour, we carefully placed everything back where we found it. Everyone appeared to be as sad as me, at the end of the adventure.

Saying goodbye to Torsten and Brenna, we waved as Mr Harris and Miss Pearce led us out of the village.

The only one of us who appeared cheerful was Brad, who finally seemed to have woken up from his daze, grabbing Theo and me, he swung around wildly.

"Wasn't that wild? A real honour fight and Torsten called me a Berserker, they are even mentioned in the history books. Maybe I am part Viking." I stared dumbfounded at Brad, unable to believe he actually enjoyed that and didn't seem at all phased by it.

"Are you mad? You challenged your brother to a duel over nothing." I couldn't let it go without challenging his comment a bit.

"It wasn't nothing, he should have said something, supported me regardless. Besides, I couldn't think of anything else to fight over."

This caused a startled reaction from Kate who had been listening in. "You did that just because you wanted to take part in a duel?"

"Yes, and it was just as amazing as I thought it would be. Fighting someone in a ring for a prize, maybe I should take up boxing or MMA."

I joined in laughing at his sudden enthusiasm for contact sports. Like most of his dreams, this one was unlikely to last any longer than when the next bright, shiny thing came along and caught his attention.

SCHOOL AGAIN

I was still buzzing over our weekend adventure, something even school on a Monday couldn't cure.

As I was getting out of the car, the bracelet on my right wrist became visible, causing my mum to comment.

"You still wearing that bracelet? It reminds me of the festivals I attended."

That caused my attention to wander and I nearly tripped as I straightened up. Ignoring the question, and quickly pulling my cuffs down, I hid the bracelet. Even though there were no rules preventing the wearing of them, this one had me concerned.

As I ran off, my mum called out as usual, causing my friends to laugh.

As was to be expected, there was only one topic in the playground, easily topping ribbing me, due to my mother calling out again.

The adventure game and weekend trip, was easily the top subject with re-enactments of our favourite plays entertaining everyone else around us, especially when the girls joined in.

Not really sure how to broach the subject of bracelets, I simply watched my friends fool around in the playground. Surreptitious glances proving to me that we were all wearing our prize bracelets.

"That gives me a problem. I can clearly remember being given the bracelet by Halvar in the game, but that is it and that was only a game."

The bell calling us to class rang and sighing I gave up wondering about the bracelet and headed into class.

As with last week, the first lesson was History and our exuberance spilled over into class at first, resulting in a noisy classroom that required Mr Harris to shout for quiet several times.

"Okay, now you have quieted down and hopefully gotten the excitement out of the way, we can get on with today's work." His smile was misleading. He was never happier than when giving us lots of work.

"I need you all to write an essay on your experience both in the game and at the adventure park. A thousand words minimum, and that includes you Jake." That caused lots of laughter and comments. My essay writing skills or lack of, were common knowledge.

"I want your thoughts on the conditions, housing, life, as well as what you actually did." He stood up, and walked around his desk and then leaned back against it.

"So some noticeable individuals over the weekend. Jake and Kate, well done on taking command without being asked and without coming over as bossy, quite the achievement."

Now he looked away from me which made me sigh in relief. It was nice to be complimented but I didn't really like the attention that came with it.

"Sienna and Jenna, well done for deciding to get extra training in, when everyone else was prepared to relax." Now he looked around the classroom, finally settling his eyes on Brad.

Along with the rest of the class, I held my breath, expecting to hear of a punishment in regards to the completely unnecessary honour fight.

"Brad, you really need to think things through before taking actions. One of these days you are going to get into real trouble." That wasn't what I had been expecting and judging by the look on Brad's face, neither was he.

"In view of my explanation of life at the time, which included a mention of honour fights, I can hardly complain when one of you requested one. Just bear in mind that they are illegal here." He paused for a moment, before continuing on in his most serious voice.

"Throughout history, the strong have at times preyed on the weak. Honour fights and similar, are easy methods of getting your own way." He paused again while looking around at us, something he did regularly to see if we were all paying attention.

"The weak, meaning non-fighters, such as bakers, tanners and especially most women, were at a serious disadvantage with this form of court. Even when allowing for the use of proxies to fight for you, that would most likely come at a cost almost as high as losing." He paused while he returned to his seat.

"Hopefully the weekend proved how much better cooperation is, to striking out on your own." Having completed his talk, Mr Harris continued on with the planned lesson.

Meanwhile, I was only half listening. My mind was still on the game and adventure park.

"It was such a great experience. More importantly, the game is available to buy and you you can attend the adventure park without school."

Thoughts of future quests and adventures filled my head for the next few weeks.

CHARACTERS

School

Mr Grumpton (Mr Grumpy), Headmaster, tall and slender
Mr Harris, Teacher, medium height, beer belly
Miss Pearce, TA, average height,
Jake, male, medium height, brown hair and eyes
Mo, male, tall, lanky, black hair, brown eyes
Vince, male, blonde hair, blue eyes
Kate, female, light brown hair, blue eyes
Jenny, female, Brown hair, blue eyes
Rob, female, Brown hair, blue eyes
Sienna, female, black curly hair, brown eyes
Brad, male, black curly hair, brown eyes, brother of Theo
Theo, male, black curly hair, brown eyes, brother of Brad

Game/Adventure

Village

Ragnar, Jarl (Chieftain)

Brenna, (Niece) blonde hair, blue eyes, twin swords, chainmail, leather jerkin, wolfskin cloak, helps adventurers

Sons, Inghram, Ingolf

Halvar, Skald, (Story teller)

Torsten, Trainer

Adventurers

Jake, male Human, medium height, Brown hair, Brown eyes, Human, Outlander, Ranger, twin swords on waist belt, small shield, chainmail hauberk; leather bracers, laced; sheepskin leather laced Jerkin; wolf skin cloak

Mo, male Dwarf, black hair, Brown eyes, Crafter, Blacksmith, war-hammer, bracers, shield, chainmail hauberk, sheepskin cloak

Vince, male, tall slim Elf, blonde hair, blue eyes, warrior, glaive and shield, chainmail hauberk, sheepskin jerkin, wolf skin cloak

Kate, tall, slim, female Elf, red hair, green eyes, Ranger, bow and short sword; chainmail hauberk, sheepskin jerkin, wolf skin cloak

Jenny, female, average height Human, light brown hair, Brown eyes, Mage Healer, bow and short sword, long skirt, chainmail hauberk, linen cloak

Rob, female, average Human, Brown hair, blue eyes, Saxon Warrior, sword, bracers, shield, trousers, chainmail hauberk, sheepskin jerkin, sheepskin cloak

Sienna, female, tall slim Elf, blonde hair, blue eyes, bard, bow, short sword, long skirt, chainmail hauberk, linen cloak

Brad, male Dwarf, black curly hair, Brown eyes, Warrior, shield and spear, bracers, shield, chainmail hauberk, sheepskin cloak

Theo, male, average Human, black curly hair, Brown eyes, Mage, quarterstaff, bracers, shield, chainmail hauberk, sheepskin cloak.

ADVENTURER'S GUIDE BOOK

Welcome to the Real Kingdoms Adventurers guidebook. Are you ready to embark on a journey through a magical world filled with mythical creatures and other fantastical elements? In Real Kingdoms, you can create your own unique character and choose to fight for a Kingdom or Clan. Your path is entirely your own and you'll engage in thrilling battles with enemies to drive them off or capture their territory.

This Guidebook gives you all the information you need to have a fun and safe adventure. It includes all the rules governing adventuring and fighting.

Included is a reference section covering races and classes. There is also a blank character sheet to allow you to create your own character, complete with back story.

THE REAL KINGDOMS

Created by Jon Abson, Real Kingdoms is an immersive real life fantasy adventure for children of all ages.

Real Kingdoms have created fun and exciting adventures days at weekends and amazing warrior camps designed to give working parents the flexibility and choice to drop off their children during the school holidays.

The children create a character for themselves and take part in a series of mini adventures throughout the year, helping them to become immersed and invested in the Real kingdoms world.

Our goal for the adventure days is to encourage children to become creative and to use their imagination.

This helps promote confidence whilst they take part in physical activities, inspiring the children to break away from their computer screens and enjoy spending time running around outdoors.

Initially working with children as a qualified secondary school teacher, Jon has become an outdoor specialist education provider for the past 15 years. Working with children of all ages, and different social and special education needs.

In RK, Jon has created a unique and highly regarded educational resource and provider, covering Oxfordshire and Wiltshire. Here primary school children come and experience life through the ages, from Stone Age to Viking.

Dressed the part in chainmail armour, will you choose to be a Warrior, fighting in large groups or maybe a Ranger acting as a scout or lone hunter.

These aren't the only choices you will have though, perhaps you are more interested in healing or crafting. There is even a Mage Class, although some other classes can also wield appropriate magic.

Create a character, the more involved the better, maybe even make your own weapons. Either way, Real Kingdoms gives you a safe environment in which to explore a new world and have fun.

Adventures await you in Real Kingdoms. Can you rise to the challenge and become a Hero?

www.realkingdoms.co.uk